Text copyright 2021 by Iain Rhys Beckett
Illustrations copyright 2021 by Graciela Tirado Orozco
Design and Layout 2021 by Rosemarie Gillen

Printed in the United States of America

Hardback ISBN 978-1-7364613-0-3

I. R. Beckett
Scribblings

Dedicated to the most noble and unselfish
parents who ever lived—thankfully they
are my own—and to every child who
deserves a happy childhood, which is
every child on planet Earth.

OSTRiCH
DREAMS

Written By
Iain Rhys Beckett

Illustrated By
Graciela Tirado Orozco

Tick-tock, tick-tock, tick-tock.

Clang, clang, CLANG!

The clock struck half-past tired.

Shadows danced in the moonlight.

ZZZ-ZZZ-ZZZ....

Snores traveled on the breeze, gently rocking
the hummingbird feeder.

"Do you hear that?" Zander spoke to no-one in particular.
"The stream is whispering!"

"Let my story begin…" the water gurgled. "
…with swift and powerful creatures."

Zander bounced excitedly, "I see ostriches!"

Stepping out from behind the giant birds, grinning boys emerged.

"Good to see ya mate!" The first lad waved.

"I'm here for an adventure," said the second.

The third stepped forward for a proper handshake, and a fourth boy declared, "Enough stand-in 'round, let's ride!"

Easily straddling the saddles, the friends prepared for take off.

"Perhaps we should toss them a snack!" suggested the first lad.

"I'm all out of crickets," said the second.

The third pulled a lizard from his pocket,
and the fourth boy announced,

"Don't ya' know, they LOVE chocolate covered strawberries?"

POOF!

A giant platter of juicy berries appeared and were gobbled down in seconds. Zander thought, Ostriches can't fly.

The stream splashed loudly and said,
"I know a secret place...."

"Show me...PLEASE!"
The boy begged.

"Off you go then!" The stream replied, rushing as swiftly
as galloping horses, leading the ostriches until they took to flight.

"Look!" The first boy shouted over the flapping of wings.

The second boy cried, "Fireflies flitting in the meadows!"

The third leaned in, squinting to make out the town street lamps.

The fourth boy howled, "Aaaahhh-Ooooooo!" into the drenching mist.

Where are we? Zander wondered.

The wind whistled, "This lake is sister to your stream,
and your island destination."

"Let's windsurf with the swans!" the first boy shouted over the current.

The second boy dipped his finger in the lake as they banked,
"YUMM!!" he grinned, "tastes like blueberry sauce!"

The third lad asked, "The kind they drizzle on cheesecake?"

"YES!" The fourth boy replied, "I smell all kinds of flavors!"

"Woo-hoo!" Zander yelled over the lake.

The lake replied, "Enjoy and have fun!
Time will escape you with the rising sun."

Bing! Bing! Bing!

Calling out over the ringing bells, the first boy said, "It's a clipper ship!"

The second boy sounded scared. "Maybe they're bad guys!"

"Maybe they're friendly," the third boy suggested.

The fourth boy asked, "May we come aboard?"

Zander spotted the captain. "You're a boy too!" he said in amazement.

"Why not, Matey?" replied the captain. "These boys are my crewmates. Welcome one and all!".

Climbing down from their feathered friends,
the boys joined in the mischief.

"Cast the anchor Mates," said the captain, as the birds took flight and landed on the island. "There's plenty of chocolate strawberries on the island to keep'm busy!"

"I'm starving too!" announced the first boy.

"I'd like cake and ice cream," said the second lad.

The third boy suggested, "How about french fries and pizza??"

"YUMMMM!" The fourth boy smacked his lips.

Zander groaned, "My tummy is growing fuller every second."

The wind whistled a reminder, "Time has flown, so you must fly!"

"Fearless friends, that's what you boys are!" said the captain.
"You'll always be welcome on my ship!"

"Thanks Captain!" grinned the first boy.

"We hate to leave, but our moms will be looking for us soon,"
replied the second boy.

"How will we find our way back?" asked the third boy as the fourth
prepared for takeoff.

"Show me...PLEASE!" Zander begged.

"Off you go then," replied the wind. Blowing mightily,
it lifted the ostriches high above the boat below,
pushing them towards the horizon.

"Look!" The first boy shouted over flapping wings.

The second boy cried, "I see the fireflies!"

The third leaned in, "There's the street lamps."

"Aaaahhh-Ooooooo!"
the fourth boy howled as they flew into the giant moon.

Where am I? Zander wondered.

"Snug in your bed," the stream whispered.

The smell of chocolate strawberries lingered in the breeze.
Tick-tock, tick-tock, tick-tock.

Ostriches have large eyes and long eyelashes, a beak that is flat and wide, and they also have nostrils. They live in various parts of Africa and their nests are in the sand.

Is it true that an ostrich will bury its head in the sand to avoid danger? No.

The common ostrich can run, at length, at a speed of 34 mph with short bursts of up to 43 mph, the fastest land speed of any bird. The common ostrich is the largest living species of bird on earth.

Common ostriches usually weigh from 139–320 lbs., or as much as two adult humans. At maturity, male common ostriches can be from 6 to 9 feet in height.

Can a human sit on an ostrich, and travel? Yes indeed. Believe it or not, in some parts of the world, humans have been known to race each other on the backs of ostriches. And yes, there is such a thing as an ostrich saddle. Ostrich-drawn carts, for example, were widely used in large cities, such as Hong Kong, in the 1870s when the British Empire covered much of the globe. These ostrich-and-carriage vehicles could even be found in the United States in the early 1900s.

9 781736 461303